Island of Horrors

Saeed Mohammed Alammari

AuthorHouse™
1663 Liberty Drive
Bloomington, IN 47403
www.authorhouse.com
Phone: 1-800-839-8640

Published by AuthorHouse 12/05/2014

ISBN: 978-1-4969-5270-7 (sc)
ISBN: 978-1-4969-5271-4 (e)

Library of Congress Control Number: 2014920220

Any people depicted in stock imagery provided by Thinkstock are models,
and such images are being used for illustrative purposes only.
Certain stock imagery © Thinkstock.

This book is printed on acid-free paper.

authorHOUSE®

To My Friends Worldwide:

I am pleased to introduce this story. I hope it is interesting and beneficial to my readers. I will feel pride if you kindly support me; your support will enhance my motivation to continue to be innovative in the art of writing. I have decided to allocate part of the income I derive from this story to support the activities and programs of Sanad Children's Cancer Support Society.

I hope you have a good time reading *Island of Horrors*.

Rayan Saeed AL ammari

It was winter; my little sister and I were sitting by the window. There was heavy rain. The winds were shaking the branches, and the lightning was flashing in the sky. My little sister was laughing and watching the cars passing. As they splashed water onto the roadsides, she shouted, "The boats, the boats!" She shouted with joy as she announced, "We have a sea in front of our house!" This, of course, made my brother and me laugh.

It was summer vacation; we were playing and joyfully watching cartoons. We were delighted as the rain continued for two days, and we stopped watching television so we could watch the rain from the windows.

From our window, we saw Dad stop his car, open the door, and come running to the house. His clothes were wet with the rain, and my little sister laughed when she saw him. Then we all laughed with happiness.

Mam told us it was bedtime and that we should drink our milk and go to our rooms. We knew that when Mam said it was bedtime, she meant it. We liked being next to the window so we could watch the cars driving through the water and people hurrying carrying umbrellas. Some people carried plastic bags or pieces of cardboard to protect themselves from rainwater. We knew that we should go early to bed.

I was half-awake and half-asleep, and I was happy. By God's will, I planned to awake whenever I liked and watch the sea in front of our house as my sister had described it. Even through the sound of the rain I could hear my dad and mam talking. Suddenly I heard my father telling Mam that a man had drowned in the tunnel as the rainwater engulfed his car. *May God rest his soul,* I thought. *He did not know how to swim, but it was God's will.* As I was falling asleep, thoughts of the drowning man in the tunnel did not leave my mind. I imagined him hitting the water with both hands, and I awoke with horror. I finally fell asleep again.

The Island of Horrors

I was standing alone on the island. There was nothing else on the island but a single tree.

The storm was raging. The wind had ravaged the tree's branches; they were nearly all broken. The wind was coupled with heavy rain. I had never seen such a storm in my life. I was standing under the tree shivering with fear, cold, and wet clothes. Strange fishes with heads like men's heads jumped out of the water. Some of them had two eyes, and some had only one eye. They jumped to reach the ground beneath the tree. The water level began to rise. I climbed the tree, yet the water level continued to rise. I started to shout for Dad and Mam to help me, but my calls were in vain. The water reached the top of the tree, and then I noticed that the strange fishes around me had large tusks.

Suddenly I saw a boat speeding toward me. On the boat was a white-haired man with a long, white beard. He appeared to be a sheikh in white dress. When he got near me, he extended his hands to save me. He took me in his boat to the land where I saw palm trees spread on a beautiful green carpet of grass. The man said, "There, behind those palm trees, is your house, but, my son, why did you not learn to swim!"

I woke up early. My two brothers were still asleep. I heard my mam preparing breakfast and tea. Dad and Mam were surprised to see me awake when I walked into the living room.

"Good morning," said Dad.

"Good morning, Dad."

"Good morning," said Mam.

"Good morning, Mam."

I turned to my dad. "I want to ask you something, Dad," I said.

"Don't tell me that you and your brothers and sister want to play in rainwater," he said.

I said, "No, I want you to teach me to swim."

"Swim?" said my mother. "What made you ask for that this very morning?"

I told her the story of the strange island. And I told them that I had heard them talking in the night. My father said, "That is really a good idea. We should teach our sons how to swim and how to ride horses. I will look for a good place where you can learn to swim during summer vacation." I kissed my father's head while dreaming of becoming the best swimmer in the world.

My father said, "If you want to learn something, you just do it." Therefore, I figured out a schedule for the remaining days of the vacation, and I started to learn how to swim. Ninety-six days remained. Each day I crossed off another day on my calendar. My little sister learned to count by looking at my schedule. Every day my father asked her how many days Rayan had left to learn to swim, and when she told him how many days had passed and how many remained, they would laugh together happily.

The Ninety-Five Days

On the day before my first swimming lesson, I woke up early before morning prayer and walked quietly into the hall where my schedule existed. My father heard me and quickly lit the light, shouting, "Who is there? Rayan? What are you doing at this time?"

I told him I wanted to cross the last day off before we left for my swimming class.

He laughed and then said, "Even if you do not write off the day, tomorrow shall be the day you begin to learn how to swim."

The day slowly passed, and I was counting the minutes and hours as I waited to go to the swimming pool described to me by my father at some hotel. Upon sunset, I started feeling some fear mixed with my enthusiasm, with the image of the drowned man in my mind hitting the water with his hands, screaming as he sank in the deep waters in the tunnel. What if I met the same fate and nobody noticed? Then I expelled that notion and imagined myself above the water moving like a fish or a boat on the river surface.

The night came, and my uneasy thoughts continued until I slept. The dreams I spent extended nights shall come true.

Day One

The long-awaited day finally came. I had dreamed for many nights of swimming. I had even carried around the swimming suit my father had bought for me. I turned the swim trunks in my hands like a valuable treasure.

We went to the hotel. My heart was beating fast as I thought about the experiment I was about to go through. I did not know if I would be successful. When we arrived, it was a beautiful moment. The lights reflected on the blue clear water of the pool. We met the coach; he was wearing a swimming suit just like Spider-Man's outfit. He greeted my father and then me with respect, treating me like a grown-up, which I liked because it made me feel secure.

Then he said, "You feel afraid, Mr. Rayan, do you?"

I wanted to say no, because I was feeling ashamed to be afraid in front of the coach, but my mother's words were echoing in my ear: "Never lie. Tell the truth even against yourself." I heard her voice inside my head as if she was speaking through a microphone. I said, "Yes, some fear."

I thanked God when the coach said, "Some fear is positive and required." Then he said, "Have you heard of the story of the two boys who were surprised by a predator in the forest?"

I said, "No, I have not heard that story."

The coach said, "Once there were two boys walking in a wood that was near their village. Suddenly they saw a predator. They were very scared, and they were certain it would devour them. One of them started running very fast out of fear. The other one, paralyzed with fear, stood frozen and screaming. The predator attacked the boy who could not run, but fortunately a man cutting wood nearby heard the screaming and rushed to the boy's aid. He used his ax to attack the predator, which went running off. That is the kind of fear that hinders and impairs us.

"You know, fear during exams, if reasonable, can be useful. It can help a pupil to work and achieve excellent marks. But if the fear is beyond the reasonable limit, then the pupil can decide that the subjects are too difficult. The pupil will wonder how he or she can study and do well. Extreme fear at exam time makes all the information in the mind forgotten."

I started feeling secure and became even more secure when the coach said, "Do you know that the human being is a swimmer by nature? If we put something at the bottom of the pool and asked you to jump in and retrieve it, you would not be able to, because the water pushes you up. Staying at the water's surface is easier than staying under water! All that you need is a little training to stay on the water's surface, and you will do that if you don't get so scared that you panic, as swimming is a natural thing for humankind."

Uncle Dahie

Within three or four days, the trainees became one family. Our fathers would chat while they waited for us, as if they had known each other for a long time. Their children became quite friendly. One person who encouraged us to be enthusiastic was a man we called Uncle Dahie. We all liked him. He had three sons training with us; one was my age, one was older, and one was younger.

Uncle Dahie used to make all of us laugh as he described the competition between us and imitated one of the football commentators: "Ahmed is fast and ahead of Fahd. Oh, a nice move! Ahmed is so close to the finish line!" That encouraged us to exert great effort and energy, because we wanted Uncle Dahie to mention our names in the presence of our fathers. As Uncle Dahie started attending the swimming competitions, some parents began bringing sweets and juices for the winners. They distributed the treats among all the competitors by the end of training.

I noticed that my father started urging me to get ready for my training, although in the beginning he used to ask me why I was in such a hurry when he thought it was too early to leave. I knew that my father liked the company of my friends' fathers, and to be truthful, we all started to fear that these good days would come to an end, we would all disperse, and we would leave each other after becoming as close as brothers.

Farewell and Dreams

On the last training day, we all lived between sadness and joy. We were happy because we had learned to swim and had made new friends. We all liked each other, and we were feeling sad about parting even though we had the most beautiful memories. We exchanged phone numbers, as did the fathers.

Dad told me, "Son, you know that knowing people is a treasure, and we are all servants of God. When we meet new people, we get to have many new experiences, and we learn new things, which benefit us in life."

The trainer gave us a warm farewell and wished us all success. I was very delighted when he said to my father, "Your son came here to learn to swim for leisure only, but he is good enough to train for competition, and we hope that, by God's will, he will be able to enter swimming tournaments." My father was delighted to hear this, and he told the coach that he would exert all his effort to make me join the best training centers for my sake and for the sake of our country.

My Mother Sets Conditions

I felt that swimming had given me many useful assets. As the trainer said, swimming gives one confidence, improves brain efficiency, encourages harmony between human organs in motion, and also improves the psychological status.

My mother was happy when my father told her about what the trainer had said. While I stood proudly in front of her, she said, "I am so happy, son, and I have no objection to you joining a training center, but your swimming should not affect your studies, which should come first."

My father asked me if I accepted my mother's condition, and with all happiness I answered, "Yes!"

I sat in the hall, remembering what the coach had said. The television was off, and my brother and sister were asleep. I still liked to watch cartoon as I used to before, but now I was looking at the blank television and dreaming. I saw myself on the screen. I was competing in a swimming tournament, and I was in the lead. Fans applauded, and I was on the platform, a green flag draped around my shoulders and a gold medal hanging around my neck. I saw myself walking down the stairs as I exited the plane. People gave me green banners, the flags of monotheism. As the flags flapped, my eyes filled with tears of joy.

"Rayan, are you weeping?" asked Mam.

I was awakened upon hearing my mother's voice. I said, "No, no, I am just happy. I got the gold medal."

"Which medal?" asked Mam.

I told her that I had been dreaming that I had been to Spain, the United States, and Italy. I said to her, "I shall know the world and the nations of the world through swimming. My father has told me that knowing people is a treasure."

She laughed and said, "Swimming has preoccupied all your thinking."

My father replied, "Let him dream. Every great deed requires a great care, and he will be hero. You will be proud of him."

Printed in the United States
By Bookmasters

Swimming has become my great dream, even though I have become more diligent in my studies to fulfill my mother's condition. It seems that my father must now resume the journey back and forth to and from the swimming training center with my little brother, Azzam, who also insists on learning how to swim. My mother says he was infected by the enthusiasm of his big brother Rayan.

My father said, "Rayan has not only inspired his brother. I also have decided to learn to swim, as there is no age limit for training." We all applaud with great interest.